The
Burst
Boiler

and other humorous stories about King Canute
and his tiny kingdom

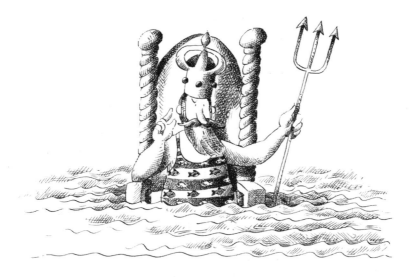

by Agnes Szudek
Illustrated by Valeria Petrone

• CONTENTS •

• • • • • • • • •

• • • • • • • • •

There was once a king called John Tostig Canute who liked to be called Canute like his famous ancestor.

This King Canute had a small and happy kingdom. In fact it was so small and not at all rich, that nobody thought of invading it. Canute had a queen called Fragmenta and two royal children. They were Prince Raglan and Princess Patchouli, usually known as Rags and Patch. He also had a bossy sister, Sophie, who often came to visit them.

The royal castle stood high on a hill. On three sides were splendid views of the leafy countryside and on the fourth there was the vast blue sea. This could be reached by descending a steep, rocky cliff.

One day, King Canute went to the east tower to find a coffee table for his sister Sophie who had arrived unexpectedly. She liked to have her favourite things at her elbow, like coffee and biscuits, tea and cakes and so on.

It was while he was selecting something from the huge hoard of collector's items with which the tower was crammed, that King Canute felt something falling on his head. Looking up, the same sort of thing fell on his face. It was a fine brown powder mixed with woody bits. The king had no idea what was wrong and went out to look for help. The head gardener was the only person in sight. He was trimming the Poodle Walk hedge.

"Ah Digweed, you're just the man I need," said the king. "There's a puzzle and a half up here in the tower. Come and see if you can solve it."

"Oh, I don't know about puzzles, Sire," said the surprised gardener, but he followed the king.

They squeezed their way up the dark steps, past furniture, ironmongery, machinery and many objects which only Canute could identify.

When they reached the top, King Canute said, "Now give me your clippers and I'll show you."

The gardener handed over his hedge clippers and the king jabbed them into one of the beams in the roof. At once a brown powder landed on the gardener's head, together with a lump of wood which had come away with it.

"Oh, sorry about that, Digweed," said the king. "But you see what I mean? Have you any idea what's wrong with the place?"

The gardener, who was not a builder, dusted his bald head and said, "I'm sorry, Sire, I only know about living wood in the garden. Dead wood's another story. But my guess is you've got dry rot. It's not much, but it could get worse."

"Dry rot?" repeated King Canute, who thought he might have heard about it before. "But that's serious, isn't it, Digweed?"

"Oh yes Sire. You'd best get it seen to before it spreads. The top of your tower could fall off."

"Oh, gracious me! And to think I only came in for a coffee table. Thank you for your excellent advice Digweed."

As they left the tower, King Canute closed the door very gently – just in case. Then he tiptoed away with the table.

When he told Fragmenta and Sophie the bad news about the tower, the queen said, "Oh Canute, it would be frightful if it fell down on the children. We must have it repaired at once, my love."

The king shook his head and sank into a chair with a long sigh.

"I'm afraid things are pretty tight at the moment. We can hardly afford our shoe repairs. I just don't know what to do. It's bad enough having the children in bed with chickenpox without the castle falling down about our ears."

His sister Sophie put down her cup and swiped the air with a sponge finger. "There is only one thing to do," she said. "Get rid of it. Knock it down before it falls down. There is no time like the present with the children safely out of the way. In any case, the tower is only full of junk as far as I know."

But the king did not agree.

"Certainly not! Stones don't get dry rot for a start and what would our ancestors think of us knocking the place about?"

"They would think nothing at all, Canute. They are dead and gone," his sister retorted.

"Dead, yes, but they have not gone far," said the king. "When I pass their portraits on the stairs, I get the feeling they

are watching us, especially Canute the First. He's got a look on his face – a kind of secret smile, if you know what I mean."

Sophie shook her head fiercely.

"I do not know what you mean," she said. "But for a king, you talk an awful lot of rubbish. King Canute's secret smile indeed!"

She rose from her chair and swept out to the balcony, leaving the king feeling small and foolish.

Queen Fragmenta patted her husband's arm and said gently, "If only great–granny's pearl box would turn up. But don't worry, we will find it sooner or later and we will be quite rich."

The pearl box to which the queen referred had belonged to the king's great-grandmother. It was decorated with pearls and said to contain fabulous jewels. It could be seen in the family portraits, yet the box had never been found after her death.

Canute was still considering his problem when Sophie advanced upon them almost at the gallop.

"I have a brilliant idea! I know exactly what we will do," she announced. "Since you will not get rid of the tower, Canute, we will open a fund."

"Open a fund?" echoed the king and queen together.

"A fund to restore the east tower, of course. We will do something spectacular to get the money rolling in, then you can see to your repairs. The plumbing needs looking at for a start. Believe me, there's going to be a severe blockage somewhere. Why this morning when I was in the bath – ."

"Yes, yes Sophie," the king interrupted. "Tell us about the spectacular thing you want us to do."

The countess settled herself down and accepted another cup of coffee, then she began.

"We will open the castle to the public," she said. "After all, your subjects have a right to see what they pay for in taxes. It will be superbly organised. We will charge for admission and simply everyone will be clamouring to get in. The cash will rise up like a mountain."

The king and queen thought it was a good idea and for once they were glad to have a visit from the mighty countess. It was decided to open the state rooms on the ground floor, the main staircase with its portrait gallery and the upper landing with the glass cases of ancient relics. Naturally, the castle gardens would be on view with the queen's own flower borders.

Sophie decided she would be the guide for inside tours. The queen offered to be the guide in the gardens and the king assured them both that he would be absolutely everywhere doing anything that was required of him.

"All the same," he added, "I think it lacks sparkle. It wants a bit of zip or zing to liven it up, don't you think?"

"Quite right, Canute," agreed the queen. "It needs a high spot, like a really good party."

"Now *I* have a brilliant idea!" cried the king, a little wildly. "The chair of Canute the First. You know, the one in the glass case on the upper landing. I will take it down to the beach and give a demonstration of its rare powers. That should be a fitting climax to the day's business."

His sister looked horrified.

"You cannot be serious. No, you cannot mean you are going to tell the waves where to go, Canute?"

"If my ancestor got the waves to lie down like good little dogs, so shall I." The king bent to pat the queen's poodle.

"You will live to regret it," his sister warned him. "I dislike that chair. I have never liked it since the first day I set eyes on it. It has a dishonest look about it. Now let us hear nothing more about that idea."

King Canute felt flattened for the second time that day.

His sister went on, "We will have roll-a-penny stalls, puppet shows, pin-the-tail-on-the-donkey – that sort of thing. We must not excite the people more than is good for them or they will be rampaging all over the place. You see, I have it all worked out."

With Sophie in charge, the king and queen left it at that and eagerly awaited their first Open Day. Still, King Canute had an odd feeling each time he passed the portrait of his ancestor on the staircase. The smile on that royal face seemed to grow wider every day.

"It's my vivid imagination, and I didn't know I had one," murmured Canute, trying not to look the painting in the eye.

As the days went by, he kept his promise and trotted about all over the place, doing every job that was asked of him. On the morning of the great day, he was so worn out and grubby he decided to have an extra long soak in the bath before the nation arrived.

Upstairs in his bedroom, he tossed off his working clothes and crossed the landing to the bathroom. He would have one en suite when the plumbing was overhauled.

The hot and cold water were gushing steamily into the bath when he thought he should have brought his watch with him. ROYALTY IS NEVER LATE was embroidered in a frame beside the bath, but it was not much good without a timepiece. So he left the water running and hurried back to his bedroom.

By the time he had found his watch and returned to the bathroom, the water had risen to the rim of the bath. He turned off the taps and reaching into the bath with his back-scratcher, he pulled out the plug. But the water did not drain away, neither through the plughole nor the overflow.

"Oh bother! The thing's blocked! Sophie warned me it would happen," he said irritably. "Never mind, let's get in."

He was about to put one leg in when he remembered a science lesson from his school days.

"If a stone is placed in a jar full of water, it will overflow. I suppose it's the same with a man and his bath water," he concluded.

For a moment he was stumped, but only for a moment. Outside on the landing was:

THE CHAIR OF KING CANUTE *(Son of Forkbeard)*
Controller of the Waves

"I'll sit on it and get the water to go back a bit," said the king, brainily. "I'll show my sister she can't always be right."

Wrapping his towel round him, he went out to the landing, took the key from behind a plant and opened the glass case. He grabbed hold of the solid wooden chair with both hands, but it did not budge. The ancient wood was heavier than it looked. By the time he had struggled to get it out on to the landing, he heard the strident tones of his sister bringing a guided tour up the stairs. Royalty was much too late!

"You will observe that Her Majesty the Great Queen Mother, dead and gone I am sorry to say, is never painted without her magnificent pearl jewellery box. There she is leaning on it. There she is opening it and yonder she is standing beside it. But alas, alas – well, I never!"

The guided tour had reached the landing. The countess paused. She glared through her lorgnette at the figure of the king in his bath towel, wrestling with Canute's chair.

When King Canute saw dozens of popping eyes upon him, he froze. Then overcome with embarrassment, he abandoned the chair and fled back to the bathroom.

He spent the next twenty minutes baling out some of the water through the window using his tooth mug – to the surprise of people passing under a cloudless sky. When at last he eased his aching bones into the water, which by then was cold, he remembered the precious chair on the landing. It could easily be taken away by someone strong enough to carry it. He groaned like a walrus and sank deeply into the water.

By the time he had soaked until his fingers were crinkled, the guided tour had buzzed off into the distance. King Canute stepped out of the bath and peeped round the door. The chair was back in its glass case. He sighed with relief and wondered whose dollop of good sense had put it away safely.

"Oh well, I'll leave it there," he said to himself. "Big sister Sophie's probably right. She always is!"

Back in his bedroom, Canute put on his best green breeches and pink jacket and sat down to sign a pile of documents that had appeared on his table.

After a good lunch on a tray and a rest with his feet up, a feeling of rebellion rose within him.

"It's high time my sister knew who's king around here," he said defiantly, strutting up and down. "Why, I am King Canute and my ancestor was a very famous man. I *shall* demonstrate his extraordinary chair. Bother sister Sophie!"

Before he could change his mind, he rang for a footman.

"Tell Digweed to take the chair of King Canute the First down to the beach for four o'clock sharp and I want it announced that everyone is to assemble on the beach at three forty-five for a special treat. After that, send along my short, formal procession."

When the footman had gone, the king threw off his finery and searched for his favourite red swimsuit, the one patterned with goldfish. He wriggled into it, swathed himself in his blue velvet cloak and put his crown on his head. He opened the door to find his short, formal procession already waiting – two for the front and two for the rear.

As they moved off slowly down the stairs, the king glanced at the portrait of his ancestor. A broad grin seemed to stretch from ear to ear.

"Oh, it must be a trick of the light," the king said to himself.

The walk to the beach was not far along a cinder track, that would one day be a decent path with scented herbs on either side. On the way, they met the gardener crunching towards them in his heavy boots.

"I've just put that chair back where it belongs," he complained. "Now I've got to get it out again."

"Ah, so it was *you*," smiled the king. "Well done, my man. Top marks for initiative. Now kindly get it out again and take it down to the beach for me."

"If you're sure, Sire. But it doesn't sound right to me." The gardener shook his head, bowed and crunched away.

It was a considerable climb down the rocks from the castle

to the beach. Most people called it a sheer drop. The king and his short procession were scratched and bruised when they reached the bottom. But the cheering and clapping that greeted Canute's appearance on the golden sand soon put a spring in his shaky legs.

Queen Fragmenta gazed fondly at the grand figure of her husband. Beside her, the countess looked troubled when she saw the gardener arriving with the chair. It was she who had instructed it be replaced in its glass case.

"Now what *is* it about that chair?" she pondered. "I cannot remember, but I am sure it is up to no good."

"Well don't ask me," said the queen. "I am not related to Canute the First. I come from elsewhere."

When the king's event was announced, the crowd chattered excitedly and arranged themselves on the sand like daytrippers at the seaside. A trumpet fanfare sounded from the castle high above and the king stepped out of his long velvet cloak. He was a glorious sight in his goldfish suit, which brought squeals of admiration and murmurs of delight from his subjects. With a dignified wave, he lowered himself on to the chair which Digweed had placed a little way into the water. Clutching the arm-rests, he sat resolutely facing the oncoming waves.

There was a hush. Even the circling seagulls overhead came to perch on the rocks. Every eye was on the monarch, expecting him to give an immediate command. But the king stared ahead in silence.

The tide crept in further and further. The water rose higher and higher until it reached the king's knees. There was a general shifting backwards on the beach and amazement at the bravery of the king. By now, his sister Sophie was so concerned she called out, "Enough of this historical nonsense, Canute. You will be swept out to sea. I have an awful feeling in my bones about that chair. Listen to me, Canute. I am older and wiser than you."

"You'll catch a frightful chill, my love," cried the queen, whose satin shoes were soaked and coming apart.

Though the king's skin had turned a chilly blue, he was determined to wait a little longer.

"I'll l-let it g-get more exciting," he told himself through chattering teeth. "Th-they deserve their money's worth, bless them all."

Well, it was when the tide had almost reached his waist that King Canute took a deep breath and bellowed:

"I command you, waves of the sea, go back into the deep. Go back I say." He raised his arms to address the briny, but the waves did not seem to understand. Still the tide came in until it covered the king's shoulders. "If it worked for Canute, it will

work for me," he spluttered nobly. But the waves did not go back.

All at once, on the crest of a huge, crashing wave, the king and his chair rose up from the sand and were spread out on the surface of the water. The people on the beach started jibbering. They scurried around in panicky knots.

The gardener was the only one to do anything sensible. He tugged off his boots and plunged into the waves.

"I'm coming, Sire! I'm coming!" he gurgled from the depths of a powerful breast stroke.

The rescue was an astounding success. In a moment, arms as strong as oaks had lifted the king high above the surging water, chair and all. Then up the watery beach came the sturdy Digweed holding aloft the king, like Neptune from his ocean bed.

King Canute's subjects, who loved their monarch dearly, were so thankful for his deliverance that they forgot the failure of the special treat.

"Long live Canute the Brave!" they cheered. "Long live our king! The noblest of them all!"

Dripping wet, but with a regal flourish, Canute waved his crown which somehow had managed to stay on his head. With cold and heavy legs, he began the rocky ascent. His subjects swarmed up the rocks behind him, cheering until they were hoarse.

Much later, when the king was wrapped in a blanket, his feet in a mustard bath and sipping hot chocolate, his sister Sophie glided in with an ice-pack on her head.

"Canute! Canute!" she cried dramatically. "It has all come back to me about that wretched chair. It had nothing at all to do with the waves. It was King Canute's favourite beach chair and nothing more than that. He always sat on it at the seaside."

"You mean – you mean –" began the king weakly. "You mean he didn't sit on it to hold back the waves?"

"Never! He failed to do that anyway. He had a go – just like you, but it did not work. I knew there was something dishonest about it. I told you so, but you never listen to me and I am always right."

The king shut his eyes, wanting to block out the thought of his public disaster. His sister began to count the day's takings with Queen Fragmenta who was too upset to say a word.

The pile of money turned out to be enough for repairs to the east tower with a bit left over for some of the castle plumbing. This pleased everyone, even the Countess Sophie.

"There is nothing like an ice-pack for clearing the brain, Canute," she said. "Remind me to tell you about it when you are back to normal."

The king gave a sickly smile to his goblet and wished his big, bossy sister would vanish into thin air – just for an hour or two. But she did not.

From that day onwards, the portrait of Canute the First somehow resumed its original expression and the dishonest chair was replaced in its glass case with a new label:

THE BEACH CHAIR OF KING CANUTE
(Son of Forkbeard)
Upon which He did not Rule the Waves.

* * *

One Saturday morning, the royal family sat down together for breakfast and began whacking the tops of their boiled eggs for all they were worth.

Clunk! Crack! Splatter! went Prince Raglan.

Ping! Pong! Slush! went Princess Patchouli.

Then BOOM! BOOM! BOOM! echoed round the room. Plaster fell from the ceiling. The chandelier skimmed the table and crashed to the floor.

The whacking stopped. For a moment there was a big, numb silence.

"How many times have I told you not to whack your eggs so hard," said Queen Fragmenta quietly.

"Oh really? Was it the eggs, dear?" asked the king, looking at the battered breakfasts. "What a relief. I thought it was more dry rot."

Rags and Patch shrieked with laughter and begged for seconds of eggs that might go with a bigger BOOM! BOOM! BOOM! But their father told them to have seconds of toast and go out to play.

The king had no time to inquire further about the trouble before another one appeared in the shape of his big twin sister Sophie who was coming to stay for a few days. She was ten minutes older than Canute and always thought she knew better than he did.

She sailed in through the double doors in a cloud of blue silk and lace.

"Oh Canute! Canute!" she cried. "I had almost arrived when I heard the most frightful noise. My coach shot right up in the air. I was sure I was going to kingdom-come, but here I am." She threw herself into a plastered chair and fanned her large red face.

"Oh don't worry about it, Sophie. It was only our boiled eggs," said the king, shaking white flakes from his toast.

His sister forgot to be polite and croaked,

"Eh?"

"Yes, yes, it was the eggs. They must have too much sulphur in them. I have thought so for some time. I shall have a word with the chicken-feeder," said the king.

By this time, many pounding feet had pounded right up to the doorway and hot, steamy faces gaped in.

"Your Majesty! Oh Your Majesty! It's the laundry. It's all gone. Blown to smithereens!"

There was an outbreak of gasps, then a royal stampede to see if this awful news could possibly be true. The stampede clattered down the stairs, raced past the stables and round the corner into the laundry yard at the back of the castle. It was true. The ancient laundry building that had stood the test of centuries was now a heap of rubble from which smoke was rising. The boiled eggs were certainly not to blame.

"How on earth did it happen?" cried the king, stumbling about among the ruins. "Are we at war and nobody told me? Have we been invaded or something?"

"Oh no, Sire. We did it ourselves. The big boiler burst. It's been threatening for donkey's years. We keep saying so. Lucky thing we hadn't put the washing in or all your socks would have gone up too. Today's sock day."

Countess Sophie, who had joined the stampede in a dignified way, wagged a jewelled finger.

"I told you already Canute, your plumbing is a disgrace. But you never listen to me and I am always right."

This was not strictly true. Most of the castle plumbing had been repaired, but not the laundry.

The king looked at the bags of washing heaped in their special barrows.

"What a wretched nuisance," he said, shaking his head. "Well, you'll just have to wash them all by hand. I'm sure that will do nicely, thank you." He tried to sound grateful, but the laundry workers stood like a solid wall.

"Sorry, Sire," said the supervisor. "No boilers, no washing. We're not allowed to do it by hand. It's against union rules."

"Is that so?" snapped the king, bristling a little. "Well, I happen to be the king. This is my kingdom and I make the rules here."

"Not in our union you don't, Your Majesty. Sorry, but sock day's off."

The laundry workers clearly meant what they said because they marched to the joinery and began to make placards. In no time at all, they were picketing the castle. Round and round they stamped. Then they went off into town to spread the bad news.

"What do we want?"

"Boilers."

"When do we want them?"

"Now!"

Such an exhibition had never been seen or heard in the land before. The king and queen were too embarrassed to look through the windows, so they peeped through the firing-slits instead.

"This is outrageous, Canute," Sophie bawled into the king's ear. "Make them do as you command or clap them in irons. Send them to the tower. Cut off their pensions. Show them what you are made of."

King Canute winced at these gruesome measures and did not reply. There always seemed to be trouble when his sister was around, even if she was not the cause of it. It had been the same when they were children. But in a moment he had cleared the decks of his brain and come up with an idea of his own. Of course – the royal family would do the laundry themselves. However, when he suggested this, no one wanted to help.

"Have you forgotten my dear, I am the queen," ventured Fragmenta, tapping her crown. "I do not know how to launder. I never learned."

"Neither did I," replied Canute, "and I am the king. But I am willing to try. It can't be difficult to get the hang of." He turned to look at his sister, but she chilled him with a frosty glare.

"Do not look at me, Canute," she grated. "I know nothing about laundry and I did not bring any." She swept away to sit in the scented rose garden.

It was not long before the king had another brainy idea.

"I have it, the very thing!" he cried. "Now is the time to teach the children something useful at home. They can wash their own socks. It's mostly their laundry anyway." He looked about and called: "Raglan? Patchouli? Where are you? Come and make yourselves useful."

He was too late. The royal children who had been there a moment before, were not in sight. They had guessed what might happen and were off to hide in their favourite hollow oak tree in the woods.

So, the king and queen were left to tackle the laundry between themselves. Fragmenta agreed to wash her own silk stockings and her bedsocks, while Canute somehow got all the children's socks to do as well as his own. He looked at the bulging bags and wondered how many he had to cope with and whether a night shift would be necessary.

Two children – that meant two pairs of socks each day and one pair each day for himself. Canute wished he had listened more carefully to his maths teacher long ago. He concentrated with his eyes shut and soon he had worked out the sum. Three pairs of socks multiplied by seven days in the week was, twenty-one pairs of socks. Or, to put it another way, he had forty-two socks to scrub, all by himself.

"Nearly enough for half a centipede," he groaned as he opened a couple of packets of washing powder.

Fortunately, he and the queen had a bathroom each with plenty of space in which to splash about. The queen filled her washbasin with hot water and poured in so much powder she was smothered in bubbles.

She was feeling hot in her royal robes, but doing her very best when she heard odd, squelching, plopping sounds coming from outside. Struggling to look through the frothy bubbles, she thought she saw nasty little heaps on the cobblestones below. She had no idea what they were.

Meanwhile, Canute in his bathroom had set to work with a nailbrush and such gusto that he almost scrubbed holes in the woolly socks. But when he rinsed them, he did not know where to put them.

"Oh bother!" he muttered. "I should have brought up some buckets. I'll just have to chuck the lot down to the garden and sort them out from there. Here goes."

Opening the window wide, he tossed the socks out one by one. But the courtyard was nearer than the garden and that was where most of the socks landed, squelching and plopping in little heaps. That is except for the ones that landed on the troopers who were changing backdoor guard at the time.

When the forty-second sock had gone whizzing out of the window, King Canute trotted down the stairs after them. He grabbed some handy buckets from the stables and stuffed the socks inside. But there was nowhere to hang them. The laundry lines had gone sky high with the building.

The king scouted among the rubble for bits and bobs he might knot together. There was nothing he could use, unless ... nearby, in a fine clump of weeds, was a sturdy-looking gooseberry bush, untouched by the disaster.

"That's what I'll use," said Canute to himself. "I'll bung the socks on that to dry. It couldn't be better."

Since the bush was surrounded by long grass and the king was not keen to step on unknown territory, he stayed where he was and flung the socks at the bush with overarm throws – like an expert bowler.

When he had finished, it was more like a sock bush than a gooseberry. Canute was thrilled with his success and was admiring the composition when a munching and smacking of lips came from one of the upper windows of the castle.

"You should not have done that Canute. It is not the way with socks. You will live to regret it." It was his big sister Sophie, giving orders as usual and chewing Turkish delight at the same time.

Canute looked up at her gnashing teeth, but he said nothing. He was stamping heavily away from the gooseberry bush, when for the second time that day he heard an extraordinary sound. This one was coming from behind him – a rumbling, crumbling kind of racket that could not possibly be Sophie.

Turning, he was just in time to see a huge hole opening up in the garden and down into it was sinking the gooseberry bush with the day's washing. Canute could hardly believe his eyes. He watched until the bush had completely disappeared as though sucked into the earth by a mysterious power. Miserably, he looked up at the window. His sister was still there.

"Now you see what you've done, Canute. For a king, you create an awful lot of havoc. First an explosion with your eggs, now an earthquake with your socks. You are not safe to have around."

There was no use reminding her that it was all caused by the burst boiler. Once his sister had an idea fixed in her head, it stayed fixed.

King Canute turned back to the unexpected hole and gingerly stepped over to it. Looking in, he could see the uprooted bush on its side with a multitude of socks scattered about. What made his stiff upper lip quiver with excitement was the flight of steps which he could see leading to a darkened entrance of some kind.

"A secret staircase," he gasped. "Nobody told me I had one of these. I wonder where it goes to?"

Without pausing to think of danger, he dangled one leg over the side, then the other and slid down until his feet were on the steps. Seven slippery steps led him to a narrow opening. Bending under the low roof, he edged his way along a dark tunnel that sloped steeply upwards until he came to a lighter part which revealed another gaping hole, right in front of his feet.

"Oh, bless my what's-it!" he gulped, stopping just in time.

The light was coming from above where he could see the blue sky he had just left behind, while from the darkness below came the murmur of voices. And that was not all. There before his eyes, although he had to strain to see it, was the last object in the world he expected to find. On a sooty ledge across the gap was a grimy, but most certainly deluxe jewellery box decorated with pearls. Could this be his great-grandmother's long lost pearl box?

Trembling and close to the edge, he stretched forward across the gap. He had just managed to clasp the box in his arms when he missed his footing and fell down the chimney, for that was where he was – in the chimney. Right down the chimney he went and tumbled into the room where Queen Fragmenta and his sister Sophie were having coffee. Prince Raglan and Princess Patchouli were cross-legged on the carpet eating buns, with butter running down their frilly fronts.

"He–e–e–elp!" Queen Fragmenta screamed at the apparition. "A demon up the chimney!"

"A chimney-sweep down the chimney, more likely," declared Sophie, popping a whole chocolate éclair into her mouth.

"No it's not. It's Father Christmas!" shouted the prince.

"Oh, early Christmas everybody!" yelled the princess. "It's early Christmas!"

They threw their buns in the air and jumped up and down on the carpet.

The sooty figure on the floor rose to its hands and knees and looked at them through black rimmed eyes.

"All wrong!" the king sang out wearily. "It's only me."

His sister looked at him through her lorgnette.

"This is the very limit, Canute, even for you," she said witheringly. "Why must you come down the chimney when there's a perfectly good staircase?"

"I didn't mean to come down the chimney," said the king finding a few bruises as he dusted himself off. "I didn't even know I was in the chimney. But it was worth it. Look what I found. It's great-granny's jewellery box full of treasure – the one that's been lost since the moon was cheese."

His sister showed no interest. She said dryly,

"It is empty, of course. The jewels have gone. You can't seriously imagine it has been sitting up the chimney unnoticed for the past hundred years."

In reply, Canute shook the box. It rattled. Desperately hoping his sister was wrong for once, he prised open the lock with a toasting-fork and took a solitary peek.

"Ah–ha!" he cried, confidently throwing back the lid. "What's all this then?" In his sooty fingers he held up: pearly rings, bracelets, brooches, tiaras and strings of pearls. They were large and priceless, small and sweet, perfect enough to please the most particular oyster – and that was only the pearly part of the treasure. Glints and twinkles promised more underneath.

Leaving Fragmenta speechless with ecstasy and his sister speechless at being wrong, King Canute carried the box to the large portrait of his great-grandmother on the staircase. Round her slim neck were coils of perfect pearls. Pearl brooches rested on her satin gown. Her hands and ears glowed with pearls and a diamond and pearl tiara circled her head. Beside her on a table was a box. It was identical to the one the king held in his hands.

The long and troublesome mystery of the jewellery box was solved.

"Oh day of joy! Now we're rich as monkeys!" called King Canute.

The prince and princess ran and knelt before their father on the stairs.

"Please, can we have parties every day and a birthday once a week?" begged Princess Patchouli.

"Can we have pocket money now and spend it on anything we like?" pleaded Prince Raglan.

"Oh, I don't see why not! I don't see why not!" said King Canute, too thrilled to be able to think clearly.

Princess Patchouli was so happy she sprang on to her ballet points with a wide beam, while Prince Raglan tried out a sailor's hornpipe he was learning. Even the king was about to dance a victory jig on the threadbare carpet when the sound of picketing blew in through the window.

"What do we want?"

"Boilers."

"When do we want them?"

"Now!"

King Canute leaned out of the window and whistled in a most unkingly way.

"I say down there! You can have them. We'll build a brand new laundry with as many boilers as you like. We've just come into a sizzling fortune."

When the laundry workers heard this amazing news, they dropped their placards and waved their caps in the air, cheering wildly.

"Good old Canute! Hip–hip–hooray! Hip–hip–hooray!"

Queen Fragmenta and the children joined in. The only one who did not join in the cheering was Countess Sophie. She was most upset at being wrong for once in her life. To cheer her up, King Canute offered to send her on a world cruise – just like Magellan, the long way round.

She accepted slowly with a suspicious look. Then the king, exhausted after a hectic washday and a spot of pot-holing, flopped into a chair and fell asleep.

* * *

One morning in summer, things were very quiet at the castle. Prince Raglan and Princess Patchouli were on half-term holiday from school and had been ordered to have a long lie-in.

King Canute had risen early and was hard at work with his councillors. They were going over the final arrangements for the visit of the Baron of Higham Ferrers who was due to arrive at ten-thirty on a trade mission.

"We must make a terrific impression on him," said the king. "He has so much money, he doesn't know what to do with it. We could soon show him, what?"

Although Canute had recently found his great-grandmother's long lost pearl box containing fabulous jewels and the odd gold coin, he was not a rich man. The jewels were family heirlooms and had to be kept in the royal family. His sister Sophie insisted on that. So Canute was as poor as ever.

"What do you think the baron will invest in, Your Majesty?" asked one of the councillors.

"Oh it could be anything, if he likes us, it could be nothing, if he doesn't. What we need most of all are jobs for everyone and repairs to the west tower. After dry rot in the east tower, we now have it in the west."

"Where does the baron's great wealth come from?" asked another councillor.

"Well, for a start he invented the parrot clock – same as the cuckoo, but different bird. Much louder. You'll notice a few hanging around, that's to impress him."

At that moment, a parrot sprang out of the clock on the wall and squawked:

"Eight o'clock precisely. Craawk! Craawk!"

"Thank you kindly," said Canute, covering his ears. "As I was saying, the baron has gold and silver mines across the seas. It is said he is one of the richest men in the world, so everything has to be absolutely perfect. If we play our cards carefully, we could see a factory or two sprouting up with jobs for all. I think everyone's finding it hard to keep the wolf from the door."

The councillors mumbled in agreement.

The king checked that three hundred metres of the best red carpeting had been laid down leading to the castle, with two dozen trumpeters on either side and a welcoming party of the noblest in the land. The queen had seen to it that the castle was beautiful inside and out. The furniture and the floors had been polished until they shone like glass and the window-cleaners were trying to finish the windows in time. The water had been changed in all the goldfish ponds and Queen Fragmenta was at that moment in the scented rose garden cutting scores of flowers to fill the vases.

The sun was shining hotly as if on royal command and Canute's big bossy sister Sophie was safely out of the way on a world cruise. Everything seemed perfect and yet ... two dark clouds were hovering somewhere.

King Canute was just thinking that if he could have any wish in the world granted at that minute, he would wish it was not his children's half-term holiday. Instead of a fairy godmother with a wand, the double doors opened and in rushed Prince Raglan and Princess Patchouli.

"Oh Dad! We've had the longest lie-in ever invented. Can we get up now?" cried the prince, sliding along the polished floor in his slippers.

"Please, Dad. It's eight o'clock. The parrot just said so. I couldn't sleep another winkle, honestly," said the princess, holding the end of her long nightgown.

King Canute groaned into his sleeve and the councillors tried hard not to. There was always trouble when the royal children were around. The king knew he would have to give them permission to get up before a pillow-fight broke out. He drew himself up to his full height and issued a stern warning:

"You will remember that today is a most important day in the life of our little kingdom. Today could make all the difference between rags and riches, even to you. I demand therefore that you be on your best behaviour, if you have any, at least until bedtime. You are to be seen but not heard. If you give me any trouble I shall personally march you to the dungeon. Is that understood?"

"Yes Dad, only we haven't got a dungeon any more," said Prince Raglan quite correctly. It had been done away with as a bad idea. "But we'll be as quiet as mice."

"We'll be so good, you won't know it's us," beamed Princess Patchouli.

"Do not forget what I say. Now off you go."

The children bowed, curtsied and tiptoed from the room. They were as good as their word. After porridge and toast, they put on their roller-skates and rattled and rolled along the polished corridors with their mouths tightly closed. Although the noise from the wooden wheels of their skates was deafening, at least it gave everyone warning to get out of the way in time.

Well, that is until they whizzed right into the butler who was coming along with coffee and biscuits for the king. The tray shot out of his hands, struck the wall and crashed to the floor, breaking all the china and the biscuits. Rags skated off for a broom to sweep up the china and Patch wiped up the spilled coffee with her petticoat. However, it was all seen by King Canute from the door of the council chamber.

Rags and Patch apologised in a whisper. It was after all an accident, but their father was in despair.

"Oh, it's no use. There's always trouble when you're around – just like someone else I know," he complained. "Take yourselves out of the castle before you have it down on our heads. Why can't you be like other children and play in the sun? Go and fly a kite!" He mopped his brow with his lace handkerchief and felt that the worries of the day were descending much too early.

"Great idea, Dad. Yes, we'll go and fly a kite," whispered the children. They bowed and curtsied again to show their good intentions and went to collect their big fish kite from the garden shed. They soon had it up in the air almost touching the fluffy white clouds that were sailing by.

It was while they were happily running about the grass, sending messages up the string of the kite on bits of paper, that they heard the sound of a horn in the distance.

"That must be the Baron of Higham Ferrers," said Rags. "Let's give him a cheer as he goes by. That should please him. Maybe he'll leave us a goldmine in his will."

"We'd better wave our crowns then so he'll know it's us," said Patch.

They stood on two high rocks overlooking the road. When the coach rolled by they jumped down and yelled:

"Hooray for Higham Ferrers! Hip–hip–hooray! Hip–hip–hooray!"

The glint of their golden crowns was caught by the sun as they waved them about like rattles. The baron was not expecting this sudden outburst in the quiet countryside, neither were the horses. They shied and whinnied with fright at the glittering objects. Then they bolted at full speed out of sight, round the leafy bend, with the coach rocking dangerously from side to side.

Now, while they had been cheering the baron, Rags and Patch did not notice that their kite had soared over the castle and was at that moment draping itself over the royal flag. Too late they saw the big grey fish lolling about on top of the flagpole. And there was nothing they could do about it.

By then, their father had changed into a fine scarlet suit and short orange cape, to cut a colourful dash. His short, informal procession was waiting outside the door. Fragmenta had just told her husband how handsome and kingly he looked when he thought it was high time the baron came into view. He took his binoculars from the shelf and scanned the peaceful panorama of his lands.

"Oh what a glorious day to entertain the baron. Oh what a glorious day for luncheon on the lawn. Oh what a glorious – what a ..." He paused as his binoculars swung over the flagpole and beheld, not the royal flag with its crown held up by a couple of ferrets, but a great big fish!

"By jove! That's odd. There's a haddock on the flagpole," he said, scarcely able to believe what he was talking about.

"A what, Canute?" asked the queen.

"A haddock, if I'm not mistaken," murmured the king, trying to focus the lenses to tell the plain truth.

"Now, now, you're over-excited my love," said Fragmenta softly. "We do not run fish up the flagpole."

The king had no time to argue. The next moment, there was a wailing and a howling and into view with a mad rush came the coach of Higham Ferrers. It said so on the doors, Higham Ferrers. It was not there long and had soon vanished, careering across the countryside, missing the castle altogether. The welcoming party were still bowing stiffly as the coach and its dust skimmed past their noses.

"Well, that's odd," said the king.

"Something *else* odd, dear?" inquired the queen.

"It's Higham Ferrers. He's been and gone and didn't even come in," said the king, perplexed.

The queen, who had learned long ago never to be perplexed, said soothingly:

"There, there. He can't have been and gone already. It must have been a mirage, like the haddock on the flagpole. You've been overdoing things, Canute. Do sit down. Have a mint. You'll feel better in a jiffy."

She gently took the binoculars from the king and looked at the flagpole herself. She glanced away, then looked again. She opened her eyes as wide as they would go. Instead of the royal standard there was indeed a great, scaly-looking fish.

The queen looked more carefully than the king. She soon saw a tell-tale piece of string dangling down over the battlements. Her quick brain told her almost immediately what it was. It was the kite she had bought for the children at Easter time to take their minds off guzzling chocolate eggs.

"I'll be back in a moment, Canute," she said. "Put your feet up for five minutes and close your eyes. I won't be long."

She hurried away knowing exactly where to find the children, in their hiding-place in a hollow oak tree.

"I don't know how you do it," she said solemnly. "If there was a prize for unruly behaviour, you would win it every time."

When the children explained that it had been a terrible accident, like the other one that morning, their mother believed them. She took her rose secateurs from her pocket and snipped the string of the kite. At once the fish, caught by a summer breeze, took off into the sky. It flew away over the forest, leaving the royal flag free to billow as it should. Then taking the prince and princess firmly by the hand, she marched them back to the castle to wash and change.

Meanwhile, it was not long before the Baron of Higham Ferrers returned – when his coachmen had calmed the horses and swung them around. The welcoming party bowed once more as the baron, this time, stepped out of his coach. He was a fine figure of a man in bright yellow jacket and breeches, a black feathery hat and adorned with jewels wherever he could wear them.

The trumpets sounded, drums rolled and the band struck up a medley of the king's favourite jigs as Canute stepped grandly on to the red carpet to meet his guest. He squinted up at the flagpole and sighed with relief at the crown and ferrets.

"Fish indeed! Silly old me," he muttered, embarrassing himself as he held out his hand to the baron.

"Welcome to my happy little kingdom," he said. "We are delighted to have you as our guest."

"Your Majesty," said the baron, bowing low, "I am honoured." He, too, was embarassed at the mad gallop and hoped no one had noticed.

Queen Fragmenta was waiting politely at the castle door with the freshly scrubbed prince and princess who were hoping that their cheering on the rocks had fallen on deaf ears.

Luncheon was laid out with much splendour on the little lawn beside the rose garden. Silver plates and goblets stood on a snowy white cloth and the servants came with many delicacies on trays, a long procession of them. The king's cheeks soon turned rosy pink with pride.

The children behaved beautifully at the table. They ate up everything they were given without the usual fuss. They did not fight over who had the bigger bit of turkey wishbone.

When they dropped their food on the ground, which was quite often, they did not scramble under the cloth to pick it up and tweak unsuspecting toes at the same time. No, they let the queen's poodle do it for them.

"What delightful children you have," said the baron, patting them on the head. He was a large man with a large voice and a large appetite to match.

"Oh, I suppose they do their best," said the king with a tight smile.

The queen could not instantly think of a truthful reply, but she was saved the effort by the sudden appearance of the butler who arrived in a fluster and put a loud whisper into the king's ear.

"Measles? What, *all* of them? Impossible. They're not children."

The loud whisper had told the king that the tea-ladies had become spotty in the face and gone down with measles.

"They must have missed it when they were children," suggested the queen. "That does make things difficult."

"I should jolly well say so," said Canute. "We had planned a scrumptious tea for you Baron H.F.; cucumber sandwiches, sugared strawberries and a magnificent cream sponge cake. My tea-ladies do a spiffing sponge the height of Everest, you know. Now what are we going to do?"

"Well, don't look at me, Canute," said Fragmenta. "Remember I learned neither to cook nor to launder. It was not part of my education."

The Baron of Higham Ferrers twisted his ten priceless rings and muttered, "I have been known to pot an egg or two for boiling, but nothing more, I'm afraid. Cooking was not part of my education either."

It looked as though afternoon tea was a lost cause until the solution came from an unexpected quarter.

"We can do the tea," cried the princess. "Cooking's part of our education."

"Yes, we do cooking on Tuesday afternoons in school and we've learned to bake spiffing sponge cakes as high as – somewhere. We could give you a lovely surprise." Raglan was very enthusiastic.

The king and queen were horrified at the idea. But the baron, who did not know the royal children, smiled expansively and clapped his hands.

"Oh, what a progressive kingdom this is," he said. "You send your children to the local school and they learn one of the most useful things in life. After all, we have to eat to live. Sire, I think you and I can do business."

King Canute glowed with pleasure for a moment, then tried to picture his children let loose in the kitchen. He was distracted by the wealth on the large fingers in front of him. His own crown had a couple of jewels missing, mislaid after the last polishing-up. Here was a mere baron who could hardly move with the weight of wealth that hung about him. He decided to humour his guest. After all, nothing much could go wrong in the kitchen he persuaded himself.

"Well, since there are no other offers pouring in," he said, trying to grin, "let's give it a go. Cook won't touch afternoon teas so there's no use asking her. It's not her side of the fence, so to speak."

"Oh, but Canute, are you sure?" said Queen Fragmenta, thoroughly alarmed. "Not the children!"

The baron remained impressed. So, while he and the king took a turn in the gardens to discuss business matters, the queen lay down on a garden bench to soothe her nerves. The prince and princess went off to the kitchen.

Now, the royal children had not told the whole truth. It was true they had made gingerbread men and jam tarts, with a good deal of help from their teacher – but nothing more. In fact, their big problem had been in keeping the dough on the table and getting the jam into the tarts. However, they were both excellent readers and they skimmed through all the cookery books on the kitchen shelves until they came to *The Perfect Sponge Cake* and "How to Bake it".

"There's nothing to it," said the prince. "We only have to do what the book says and – hey presto!"

"Cucumber sandwiches are easy peasy," said the princess. "We can do them with our eyes shut. What do we need for the sponge, Rags?"

The prince read:
flour
butter
castor sugar
2 eggs fresh as possible
salt
And for the cream:
butter
icing sugar
Orange or lemon juice to flavour

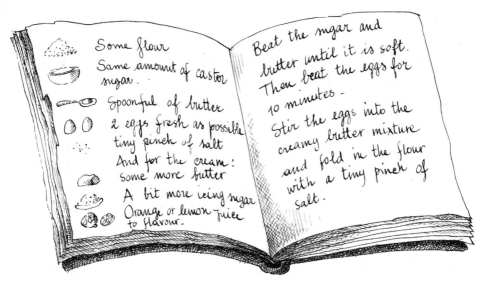

Some flour
Same amount of castor sugar.
Spoonful of butter
2 eggs fresh as possible
tiny pinch of salt
And for the cream:
Some more butter
A bit more icing sugar
Orange or lemon juice to flavour.

Beat the sugar and butter until it is soft. Then beat the eggs for 10 minutes - Stir the eggs into the creamy butter mixture and fold in the flour with a tiny pinch of salt.

The princess weighed out all the ingredients carefully. She went to the chicken-run for two eggs, so fresh they were still warm. Patch beat the sugar and the butter until it was a soft yellow cream. Rags beat the eggs for about ten minutes, as the book said. After that they stirred the eggs into the creamy butter mixture and folded in the flour with a tiny pinch of salt. It seemed exactly right as they divided the mixture between two cake tins and put it in the oven to bake for forty minutes.

They had done it as easily as if they had been baking all their lives.

"Oh Rags," cried the princess happily. "Mum and dad are going to be so pleased with us for once. Just wait till they see our sponge."

"And the Baron of what's-its-name will be so impressed, he'll give dad everything he wants," said the prince. "And all because of our sponge cake."

They were thirsty after their spot of baking and they drank a small jug of orange juice which they saw in the pantry. There was also a large bowl with red strawberry blobs inside it but no strawberries. This reminded them they had to pick fresh strawberries later and toss them in sugar. First they chose a ripe cucumber from the garden frame and Rags sliced it while Patch cut the bread.

She had never cut bread before or she would have known not to use a cottage loaf, the one with the round extra bit on the top. The best she could do without practice were thick doorsteps that used up all the loaf, so she had to cut a second one.

Rags' cucumber slices were on the chunky side too. When the tops were put on the sandwiches, they were like high, wobbly towers.

"Never mind," said the prince. "Who's going to notice when they see our sponge cake?"

It was when they had balanced the doorsteps on a plate and put them on the tea-trolley that they realised they did not know when they had put the cake in the oven.

"How will we know when it's ready?" said the princess. "I can't guess forty minutes, can you Rags?"

The prince could not guess forty minutes either. Although there were clocks all over the castle, there was not one in the kitchen.

"I know," said Rags after a moment. "There must be a cake-timer here somewhere. Quick, let's find it."

They looked in all the drawers and in all the cupboards they could reach, but they found nothing more than a three-minute sand egg-timer. Rags turned to the recipe again and read:

"Do not overbake your sponge or it will lose its moisture and be quite spoiled."

"We can't have it spoiled. It's got to be perfect!" wailed the princess.

There was only one thing to do. They would have to look in the oven and see how the sponge was coming along.

Now, if you have ever baked a cake, especially a sponge cake, you will know that is exactly what you must never do. But Rags and Patch did not know this. They opened the oven door and looked inside.

"There you are – perfect," said Rags triumphantly. "It's as high as you-know-what, but it's not ready yet. It's got to be golden brown."

"Then it'll be ready by the time we've made the tea," said Patch excitedly. They closed the door of the oven.

They had seen the tea-ladies brewing tea so often, they knew exactly what to do. At least that was no problem.

But when they went back to the oven to take out the cake, they had to look hard to find it. Their perfect sponge was lying in the bottom of the cake tins as flat as two pancakes.

For once the prince and princess were speechless. They had no idea what had gone wrong. The cookery book did not tell them.

"It's not only flat, it's as hard as a brick," said the princess, hitting it with a spoon. "What happened to it?"

"Don't ask me," said the prince glumly. "But we'll be in real trouble."

In the fearful silence of the kitchen, they heard somewhere in the castle the screech of a parrot telling them it was four o'clock precisely. There also came the clickety-clack of their mother's dainty shoes on the stone floor. The kitchen door opened and Queen Fragmenta's worried face peeped in.

"How is tea coming along my dears?" she asked a little anxiously.

"It's er ... It's er ..." said Rags, hastily standing in front of the trolley.

"Oh wonderful! Wonderful!" cried the queen, wanting to believe she had heard something else.

"That's such a relief. Higham Ferrers can't make up his mind about anything. Your poor father has walked him round and round the west tower until he's quite giddy, but the baron doesn't take the hint. He's odd, if you ask me – or a fraud. But a scrumptious tea might just do the trick. Make sure it's quite delectable, won't you?"

"Oh er ... Oh er ... " said Patch weakly and a helpless whimper slipped out by mistake.

When their mother had clickety-clacked away, the prince and the princess looked disaster in the eye and it was worse than they had thought.

"Oh look, Rags," sniffed Patch. "We've got two bricks and we've got no cream to sandwich them together. We forgot to make the cream."

They had indeed forgotten and anyway they had drunk the orange juice which was meant to flavour it. And they had not prepared a bowl of sugared strawberries.

At that moment they heard a long:

"Yoooooo–hoooooo!" echoing along the corridor. It was their mother's way of telling them to hurry up.

"Wait! I've got it!" said Rags, clicking his fingers. "Where's that tissue paper we saw just now?" He rummaged in a drawer and brought out a stack of neatly folded white tissue paper.

"What's that for?" asked Patch.

"We'll stuff it in and pretend it's cream,"said Rags, scrunching it up.

"But they can't eat paper, Rags. They'll know it's not cream. Are you mad?"

"They can't eat the cake either," said Rags, pressing the paper between the two sponge halves. "We've got to get them to eat up all the sandwiches and they'll be too full to eat anything else."

After these brilliant preparations there was nothing to do but take the tea-trolley to the rose garden and be ready, if necessary, to face the music. Trembling, they set off.

The trolley load looked much worse out in the strong sunshine. The sandwiches collapsed with all the jogging about and had to be stood up again. Queen Fragmenta was cooling herself with her silk fan; King Canute was studying the sun as it crossed the sky, without a single agreement in his pocket.

The councillors, who had been dodging about in the shrubbery hoping for a bit of good news, edged closer, pretending to smell the roses.

Only the Baron of Higham Ferrers had his eyes firmly fixed on the trolley. As it stopped, he circled it thoughtfully, with one finger tapping his mouth.

"Er – tea is served," said the princess, with a third-rate curtsey. "Would you like it with milk, Mr Baron, sir?"

"I would indeed, Princess Patchouli. What a veritable feast you lay before us."

At that point, the eyes of the king and queen beheld the veritable feast and seemed ready to pop out of their heads.

"Good gracious!" gasped the king in astonishment at the towering sandwiches, most of which were curling up in the heat and falling over again. The queen fingered her pearls and half rose to her feet, not knowing what to say.

The Baron of Higham Ferrers having scrutinised the sandwiches and bent low over the sponge, began to gurgle in his vast throat. The gurgle came into his mouth with the loudest laughter that had ever been heard in the kingdom. Then, to the disbelief of those present, he lifted the top off the sponge cake and whacked himself over the head with it. Clunk! Clunk! Clunk! it went. After this, he blew the tissue paper up into the air.

Queen Fragmenta, who already thought the baron was odd, was numbed by these unspeakable capers and began to faint very slowly sideways. King Canute caught her just in time with one arm and shook his fist at the children with the other.

Rags and Patch were frozen to the spot. They had been ready for trouble, but nothing like this.

Still the baron went on laughing.

"Oh Brillo! Brillo!" he guffawed. "What clever children you are. It's as plain as the nose on my face." He said this while donking the end of his considerable nose with the sponge. "Oh you are crafty, Sire. You have your children well trained."

"Have I?" uttered the king, confused to a great degree.

"Here I am, dithering all day long and your clever children have made up my mind for me."

"Have they?" the king said bleakly, unable to make sense of anything and feeling the weight of the queen who had not yet come round. He watched as a jewelled finger jabbed at a cucumber sandwich and a deep voice sang out in a low bellow,

"The castle tower is falling down, falling down, falling down, the castle tower is falling down ..." The baron was singing to the tune of 'London Bridge is Falling Down' but clearly he meant the west tower, which Canute had been trying to draw to his attention for hours.

"And here we have a cake as tough as leather," the baron roared. "I know what you mean, Sire. You want a boot and shoe factory. Then you shall have it, with jobs for all your people. Am I right?"

The king, who was now on the grass beside his queen, nodded vacantly, displaying his worn-out soles.

"Oh you have taken the words right out of my mouth," he said. "I could not have put it better."

The baron once again patted the heads of the children.

"Oh what it is to have a genius or two in the family."

For a moment, the children found it hard to believe that disaster had somehow turned into success without any help from them. But they recovered quickly.

"And we can dance," said the first genius. "I do the hornpipe."

"And I do the ballet," said the second genius.

Before either of them could show off their skills, the butler came along with another loud whisper for the king's ear. The measles had been a false alarm. The tea-ladies had gorged themselves on a big bowl of strawberries and come out in a pink rash. However, all was well. They were at that very moment in the kitchen preparing afternoon tea.

"Oh day of joy!" cried the king, leaping into a favourite jig. "We've just had a very successful pretend tea, now let's have the real thing."

He gallantly gave Fragmenta his arm and by the time they had arranged themselves on the garden chairs, another tea-trolley appeared with exactly what they had expected in the first place: delicate cucumber sandwiches, a perfect sponge cake the height of anything you like, a bowl of sugared strawberries, all washed down with the best afternoon tea.

Later that evening when the sun was setting behind the castle walls, the royal family waved from the battlements as the Baron of Higham Ferrers drove off in his coach. He had promised there would be work for everyone in the tiny kingdom as soon as possible.

"What wonderful children you have been today," smiled Queen Fragmenta, giving each of them a hug. "And where this stupendous idea of yours came from, I shall never know."

"Oh, we didn't really –" began Raglan and Patchouli at the same time, anxious to tell the truth.

King Canute held up his hand.

"Not another word," he said. "The secret is yours. All I will say is, thank goodness it was your half-term holiday. I could not have wished for anything more."

* * *

Early one morning when the rain was running in rivers down the castle walls, a dripping pigeon post arrived at exactly the same time as the seven o'clock parrot. King Canute was fast asleep when a sprinkling of cold water moistened his face. He opened one eye to see the pigeon coming to rest on his bed-post and the parrot springing out at him from the wall.

"It's like living in an aviary," growled Canute. Wiping his face on a corner of the sheet, he took the soggy letter from the bird. It was from his big sister Sophie.

Dear Brother Canute

I have now seen how half of the world lives and I am about to view the other half.

I shudder to think how you have managed without me all this time.

I assure you of my fullest attention on my return, which should occur soon after you receive this letter.

Your wise and ever affectionate,

Big sister Sophie

"Soon? Soon?" Canute addressed the pigeon. "How soon? When did you set off and from where? How long on the wing?"

The pigeon, which, of course, was not a talking bird, blinked its round eyes, sank its neck on its chest and went to sleep.

The king tottered to the window and grimaced through the pelting rain. He half expected to see his sister descending from her coach and shrieking at the weather, but thankfully she was not in sight. Fervently hoping she was at least a quarter of the world away, Canute climbed back into bed and rang for his tea and toast.

Afterwards, he showed the letter to Queen Fragmenta who was always a little nervous of her loud sister-in-law, although she quite enjoyed her company. The king then pulled on his rainboots and oilskins and went down to the courtyard. Braving the worst of the weather, he set to work directing operations.

This was the day that work was to begin on repairing the roof of the west tower. The Baron of Higham Ferrers had kept his promise and was footing the bill for everything thanks to a pile of cucumber sandwiches.

It seemed to Canute no time at all since the east tower had been restored. That was thanks to Sophie's brilliant idea of opening the castle to the public, but she was such a botheration, life was much easier without her. Canute was anxious that the work on the west tower should be completed before her return.

The king found there was no shortage of workers. Clusters of eager people were squeezing through the castle gates in response to his advertisement in the market square. Their heads were covered with hats, coats or sacking against the downpour. Apart from needing jobs, Canute's subjects loved their monarch and were always ready to rally round in times of need. They were in a jolly mood in spite of being drenched.

"Morning, Your Majesty."

"Out for a swim, Sire?"

"Anything you like, Your Majesty: humping, dumping, pumping, thumping. Say the word and we'll be at it."

Although Canute was grateful for their enthusiasm, he could not find work for all of them. Those who were turned away were promised months of hard work on the boot and shoe factory which was to begin shortly.

The first thing to do was to empty the tower. The king had soon organised a human chain to hand along the odd assortment of objects that had been stored inside, mostly thick with dust and cobwebs.

He was reversing out of the narrow doorway with an old tin bath when Queen Fragmenta appeared beside him, hidden under a cloak and umbrella.

"Have we started yet, Canute?" she asked pointlessly.

"Not yet, my love. As you see, we're clearing the tower. But where we shall put this priceless stuff, I do not know. We can't leave it out in the rain."

"Priceless, is it Canute? I thought it was bric-a-brac. The jig-ma-junk you bring home from wherever it is you find it. A good soaking might do it a power of good." She drew an X in the dust with her finger.

Canute was well known for the things he picked up here and there. His coach was often crammed with items he had spotted on a jaunt or even on a state visit. The odd table or chair that had been abandoned by the wayside was sure to find a good home with Canute, a ladder with no one to climb up it, a window with no one to look out of it, a tin bath with nobody in it – they all found refuge in either the east or the west tower of King Canute's castle. It was only in such a moment as the present that the extent of his hobby could be seen.

As the courtyard began to look more like a junk yard, along came carts laden with new timbers to repair the roof of the tower. The confusion and noise was too much for Queen Fragmenta. She squelched away to order a non-stop soup service for the workers, saying,

"If they don't get something hot inside them, they will die of the raindrops!" as if she had discovered a new disease.

After this, she returned to her sitting-room to play card games with Prince Raglan and Princess Patchouli who were forbidden to put their noses out of the windows or the doors without their father's permission.

An hour or so later, the rain eased off and the sun appeared. Spirits rose. The workers burst into happy tunes, singing, humming and whistling as they cleared the dry rot from the tower, throwing the damaged timbers to the ground with strict instructions to avoid the priceless collection. Canute was up his rescued ladder – a happy ruler, close to his people. It was all going with a splendid buzz.

But of course, it was too good to last. When the time came to carry the new timbers up to the roof, the workers found it impossible to manoeuvre the heavy wood up the dark, narrow steps of the tower.

"How was it done before, Your Majesty?" asked the foreman. "I mean in the east tower."

"Ah, that was simple," said the king. "We only needed a few short beams. This is a much bigger pickle. Let me think."

He sat on the upturned bath and closed his eyes. To his annoyance, he could only wonder what his sister Sophie would say if she had been there. Her head was always full of ideas.

"Oh bother sister Sophie!" he cried aloud, forgetting he was supposed to be thinking. In another moment, he had an idea of his own.

"I know what we'll do," he said, astounding himself with his speed of thought. "Siege towers! You know the things that were used long ago when everybody was invading everybody else. A superior ancestor of mine had a couple. They should be lying about somewhere."

The workmen helped him to search the grounds and the two siege towers were found in the orchard, almost hidden among the medlar trees. The inside steps had crumbled away and the towers did not have wheels, so it took some time to move them round to the west tower.

The effort had been supreme. Unfortunately, the idea fell flat. The towers were too short. They did not reach to the top of the west tower.

"I can't understand it," said Canute in disbelief. "You can't lay siege to a castle if you can't get over the wall. Even with wheels on they wouldn't be tall enough to use in a war. Are there any other ideas floating around?" he asked hopefully.

But there were no other ideas. A disappointed lull hung over everything as the work came to a standstill.

All this time, inside the castle Prince Raglan and Princess Patchouli were sullen and fidgety with boredom. They had played every card game their mother could think of and were longing to be part of the exciting work outside. But their father did not trust them running loose. It was not that he doubted their brain-power, but it was the mischief to which they sometimes put it that worried him.

The prince and princess had just invented a card game which they called 'Rapatch', when they thought they heard their father shouting:

"Raglan and Patchouli." But when they looked through the window, he was gazing elsewhere with one hand cupped to his ear.

King Canute had actually shouted,

"Ropes and pulleys" – a brainwave he had for lifting the timber, when, at the same time, his sharp ears detected a completely new sound. It seemed to be coming from beyond the grey horizon. It was not exactly a caterwauling and certainly not any known musical note. It was more like a trumpet trying not to be a trumpet, or something else that thought it was a trumpet.

"Bless my socks! What on earth is it?" Canute asked himself and rushed back up the ladder to get a better look. "Are we being invaded after all these years?"

"It looks more like some kind of creature, Sire," said the foreman who had climbed up his ladder. "Now, if I believed in dragons, I'd say it's a great big man-eating dragon and it's on its way over here for a feed."

"No, no, no, my man! We don't believe in dragons nowadays," said Canute impatiently. "Or – er – do we?"

The sun was slanting on the mysterious thing so that the front of it glittered and sent off flashing, rainbow-coloured lights.

There was a clattering of armour as the captain of the guard rushed up.

"Sire! Sire!" he called up the ladder. "A strange object approaches which cannot be identified. I fear it may be a castle wagon with a hidden army of invaders."

"You mean like the wooden horse of Troy?" asked Canute.

"Exactly, Sire. You must take cover at once and everyone with you before we're overrun. I'll order the men to their posts."

Canute came almost headlong down the ladder and dashed into the castle. Queen Fragmenta and the children had heard nothing, with the doors and windows closed.

"Fragmenta, my precious queen! Oh, my dearest children!" gulped Canute, out of breath. "This is a day of disasters. At this very moment, a most hideous thing approaches the castle. You must remain here in safety until the danger is past!"

"And how hideous is this thing, Canute?" asked the queen, putting down her cards.

"I'll tell you in a jiff." Canute grabbed his binoculars from a shelf and looked out of the window. His hands were shaking, but he was able to make out the long, suspicious shape of the thing crawling along between the trees. There was no doubt about it, it was on its way to the castle.

"Oh mercy upon us!" he cried. "It is a castle wagon. I see its roofs; I see its flags. And ... and it's drawn by a monster with two heads. Alas, I fear we may be too late to save ourselves."

"I've never seen a monster with two heads," said Fragmenta evenly. "Or a castle wagon for that matter."

"Well you soon will. Get behind the screen all of you and don't move a muscle."

"Oh but Dad, please can I go and slay the two-headed monster?" begged Raglan, eager to show what he was worth.

"And I'll help him," offered Patchouli, not wanting to be left out. But the king hustled his family out of sight, muttering,

"The gates! The gates!" He shouted out of the window for the gates to be closed, but there was no one to hear him. The workers were in hiding; the guards were at their posts and yet no one had closed the gates. 'Have my loyal guardsmen deserted me in my hour of need?' Canute wondered.

He was in despair. All seemed lost. Then above the trumpeting racket, the jingling of bells, the groaning and creaking of the enemy at the gates, he heard another sound. It came as though in a distant dream. A loud, familiar voice sang out:

"Can–u–ute? Are you there? Come out, come out wherever you are. It is I. It is So–o–phie!"

"It's impossible," said the king from his hiding-place. "Did it say – Sophie?" Fragmenta nodded, wide-eyed.

"It's big aunt Sofa! It's auntie Sophie!" cried the children who loved their noisy aunt although they were a little afraid of her.

When the royal family looked down into the courtyard, the sight that met their eyes took their breath away. It was not one beast with two heads that Canute had seen, but two beasts with one head each. They were magnificent elephants with caparisons of rich embroidery, jewels, tiny mirrors reflecting the sun and jingling bells hanging at their sides.

From the first wagon, the head of the Countess Sophie leaned out, arms waving and teeth flashing.

"I am back, Canute. I am back from my world tour and from here it looks as though it's not a moment too soon. Your castle's falling down again and I can't get through the gates for rubbish."

By now, King Canute was too exhausted even to sigh as he went out to greet his sister. 'How is it,' he wondered, 'that she happens to arrive when part of the west tower is missing and the courtyard is choc-a-bloc with my priceless collection?'

"Ah, Canute! Canute!" she cried, throwing herself into his arms. "What a dear, dear brother you are to send me all the way round the world. It will take me years to tell you everything I have seen and done. I have presents for all," she added, as the prince and princess ran to hug her. "But tell me, Canute, do you like my elephants?"

"Charming," said Canute lamely. He already felt so overcome by the day's events, he was not able to be overcome by anything else – even elephants, although he had never met one before. "Where did you find them?" he asked, avoiding a curious trunk.

"India. They are on loan. I have to send them back to my friend the Maharajah when they have had a good rest. Ah, Fragmenta, here's a hug for you." She enveloped the queen who had not dared come further than the door. "Now let us have a cup of tea. I have brought a special kind from China."

It was while they were drinking blossomy jasmine tea that Canute explained the trouble with the west tower.

"And how do you expect ancient siege towers to be in good order after centuries?" Sophie asked scathingly. "But your worries are over. I am here and I intend to stay with you for a few days."

At these words, Canute managed an old, familiar groan. Sophie had an idea. He could tell by the wild brightness in her eyes as she swallowed four marzipan cakes, one after the other. Her imagination worked better when she was chewing, she always said.

"I am quite sure it can be done easily," she declared at last. "Ruby and Emerald will help. They are dear, sweet animals and will do anything I ask of them."

She was referring to the elephants. So, after they had been fed, watered and their rich coverings removed, big sister Sophie took charge.

"Let me see these siege towers you speak of," she said. Canute showed her the two wooden towers standing idle, while the workers shuffled close to watch the mighty countess.

She examined the towers inside and out and tried to look underneath.

"They have no wheels, Canute, because they never had any wheels. They are not quite what you think they are. Now, bring me some good stout strapping, long enough to go round the elephants. Well, don't stand gaping at me, do as I say."

She was taking everyone so much by surprise that even Canute forgot he was the king and trotted off to the stables. He found several long leather straps, which buckled together would be long enough for both animals. When he returned, Sophie had ordered the wooden towers to be lifted on to the elephants' backs. Canute could hardly believe his eyes.

"Up Ruby! Up Emerald!" she was saying. "Good girls."

On command, the elephants were slowly and carefully rising to their feet.

"Oh dear! Won't they come tumbling down?" asked Canute concerned, yet secretly hoping they would.

Sophie gave him a cold stare and ordered the strapping to be slotted through the lower part of the towers.

"Now," she said, "buckle it round their tum-tums."

The towers did not come tumbling down. They sat squarely and firmly on the elephants' backs as though they had been specially made for them. And when the workers stood their ladders up inside the towers, the intelligent and willing animals swung the long timbers up to them in their trunks, as though the wood weighed nothing at all.

The re-roofing of the west tower had begun.

"All that was required was a brilliant idea," said Sophie, looking very pleased with herself.

"Hooray for Countess Sophie's brilliant idea! Hooray!
Hooray!"

Cheering and clapping rang in the king's ears. He began to
have that squashed feeling which he often felt in the presence
of his sister. He wished another hole would mysteriously open
up for him as it had once before. Sophie had done it again.
She had come up with a brilliant idea. 'Maybe she should be
king,' he thought. Even his children joined in the cheering.

"Oh clever Auntie Sophie!" shouted Rags, drumming his
feet on the cobblestones.

"Dad says you're always full of big ideas," called Patch.
"Please can we have a ride on your elephants?"

At that moment, Queen Fragmenta ventured out of the
castle.

"Oh Sophie!" she exclaimed. "How do you think of such ingenius ideas? You are so clever."

"Oh well," Sophie whispered, "it was not my idea at all. It was done in the Crusades, you know."

"What was done in the Crusades?" asked Canute of the sharp ears.

"Oh er – why, elephants holding up siege towers, of course. The Saracens did it, not I. You don't think I was at the Crusades, do you? Remember, I am only ten minutes older than you, Canute. On my way home, I read and learned all there is to know about elephants. Which reminds me, we will now unpack the wagons and you will be amazed at the things I have brought back."

They were indeed amazed. She had brought: silks and satins from China, shadow puppets from Java, wood carvings from India, rugs and rare games from Persia, porcelain from France and the wonderful castle wagon itself which she had picked up in Bohemia.

By the time the wagons were emptied, the inside of the castle was as heaped up as the courtyard and it was beginning to rain. Canute, whose smile had been growing wider by the minute, said jovially,

"I say, I've got a brilliant idea if anyone is interested. Now that the wagons are empty, I could put my priceless collection into them, out of the rain, until the tower's finished. What d'you say, Sophie?"

Sophie looked displeased but she agreed reluctantly. She had thought the pile of rubbish in the courtyard was to be thrown away. By this time, Canute was happy enough to ignore her remarks. For once it had not been Sophie's own idea that had won the day, and he was not going to let her forget it.

Canute was so delighted with the way things had turned out, he gave a grand dinner in honour of his sister's safe return. Throughout the evening, when she became too bossy and overbearing, he called out,

"Hooray for the Saracens' brilliant idea. Hip, hip –" And everyone responded.

It did not bother Sophie much, but it did King Canute a wagonload of good.

* * *